THE
BLOODWIN CODE
EPISODE #3

THE BLOODWIN CODE
is
BLOODWIN CHRONICLES
Volume One

Angela Brownemiller

BLOODWIN CHRONICLES: VOLUME ONE

THE
BLOODWIN CODE
EPISODE #3

THE BLOODWIN CODE
is
BLOODWIN CHRONICLES
Volume One

Dr. Angela Brownemiller

Metaterra® Publications

Metaterra® Publications
The Bloodwin Code: Episode 3

[The Bloodwin Code Episode Books form
Bloodwin Chronicles, Volume One]
Copyright © 2020, 2021. 1998, 2010, 2013, 2014, 2015, 2016, 2017, 2018, 2019.
Angela Brownemiller / Angela Browne-Miller.
Copyright © 2021, 2020, 2000, 1998, Metaterra® Publications.
All rights reserved in all formats and in
all languages and dialects known or not known at this time.
Published in the United States by Metaterra® Publications.
www.Metaterra.com   www.Amazon.com
Library of Congress Cataloging-in-Publication Data.
Brownemiller, Angela.
THE BLOODWIN CODE: EPISODE 3
BLOODWIN CHRONICLES COLLECTION, Volume One
Angela Brownemiller/
1. Science Fiction. 2. Psychological Thriller. 3. Romance.
4. Consciousness. 5. Psychology.
6. Angela Brownemiller. 7. Angela Browne-Miller.
8. Dr. Angela.
ISBN-13: 978-1-937951-24-5 (paperback)
See also Amazon and website below for Ebook and Audiobook.
Published in the United States of America for U.S. and worldwide distribution.
Metaterra® Publications, Metaterra.com.
Bloodwin Code by and copyright © Angela Brownemiller.
Cover and all content, text, titles, illustrations, charts, diagrams, etc.,
by and copyright ©Angela Brownemiller.
Book and cover design by and copyright ©Angela Brownemiller.
Ordering information and bulk ordering information available through:
Amazon Paperback, Kindle, Amazon Audible, etc.
Metaterra.com   DrAngela.com

****

****

*Dedicated to those
who have a right to know
who they truly are.
Everyone.*

BLOODWIN CHRONICLES: VOLUME ONE

Meet the…

THE BLOODWIN CODE - EPISODES
by Angela Brownemiller....

WHO IS WRITING THIS PLAYBOOK FOR US?
WHO ARE WE? DO WE REALLY KNOW?
WHERE DO WE DRAW THE LINE
BETWEEN SANITY AND OBSESSION?
BETWEEN LOVE AND MADNESS?
WHO HERE CAN WE TRUST? OURSELVES?
WITH OUR BODIES, WITH OUR MINDS?
DO ROMANCE AND SEX HAVE
THE SAME MEANING ANYMORE?
BE CAREFUL WHO YOU FALL IN LOVE WITH.
ARE THERE CLONES AMONG US?
ARE WE DEALING WITH LIFE FORMS WE HAVE
NO WAY TO KNOW ARE HERE?
Is this obsession or invention? Is this right? Is this wrong?
Does anyone anywhere know anymore?

This book, THE BLOODWIN CODE: Episode 3, is the third episode book in THE BLOODWIN CODE set of episode books. This is a riveting and disturbing, confusing and revealing, story of sexual and scientific intrigue, a romantic and psychological sci fi thriller, a tale of biotechnology gone wild, or running awry, or perhaps doing exactly as it should be doing, waking us up to its true nature:

Global conditions are reaching into all our lives, and into our hearts and minds, even into our bedrooms. Even those investors and inventors most directly responsible for all this out of control situation are being hit. Here in this Episode 3 Book, even love and sex are no longer what we thought these were. Even we are no longer who we thought we were. Check this page turner out. See if you can ever love again. See if anyone, or even the world, will ever look the same again.

BLOODWIN CHRONICLES: VOLUME ONE

ABOUT THIS COLLECTION OF EPISODES

This book is
The Bloodwin Code: Episode 3

The Bloodwin Code
story is told in a
series of episode books.
You will find each episode book numbered this way:
THE BLOODWIN CODE
Episode #1 Book, Episode #2 Book, and so on.

The **Bloodwin Code Episodes**
form together the first volume of the
BLOODWIN CHRONICLES COLLECTION,
therefore are together titled
BLOODWIN CHRONICLES, VOLUME ONE:
THE BLOODWIN CODE

BLOODWIN CHRONICLES: VOLUME ONE

THE BLOODWIN CODE. Episode #3

TABLE OF CONTENTS

NOTE TO READERS
REGARDING
THE BLOODWIN CHRONICLES COLLECTION

Dear Readers,

The names and events described in this BLOODWIN CHRONICLES COLLECTION of books have been fictionalized to protect persons (lay persons, students, scientists, business persons) involved in modern day human cloning research and development. A particularly special effort has been made to maintain the anonymity of those involved in seeing that such development adheres to the highest of ethical and moral standards.

Many of the situations, problems, and moral dilemmas presented by human cloning and described on the following pages definitely do exist in our times. Look around carefully, study the people you know or think you know, be aware of strangers you see in public places and at the higher levels of businesses and governments. You may find you know more about all this than you think.

Readers who prefer to read all this as fiction will be pleased to know the following story is indeed written as fiction, as a science fiction, psychological thriller, international intrigue, and yes, also in some way a romance story. Any resemblance to persons living or dead, and to clones living or dead (and imagined or actual), is entirely unintentional.

Readers who may be human clones, or hybrids, or human replicants of some sort, will please know that the following story does not intend to depict all such clones, hybrids, and replicants as morally confused or morally wanton, or as just plain morally void. Many clones, hybrids, and replicants of humans are fine human beings (if you please will allow them into the human race), and exhibit the highest of moral standards.

Human clones, replicants, hybrids, and other biologically and genetically engineered beings, as your populations finally emerge into public view, you will, I am sure, have ample opportunity to demonstrate your character, and your value to human existence. Make this value known. Or risk becoming an endangered species even before becoming a recognized species.

The Author

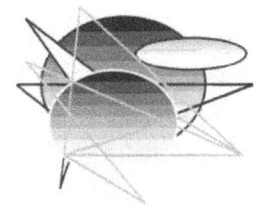

THE BLOODWIN CODE

EPISODE 3

This book, The Bloodwin Code, Episode 3 Book, follows the previous book, the Episode 2 Book. The chapters in this Episode 3 Book are numbered to follow the chapters in the Episode 2 Book. Therefore, the Episode 3 chapters begin with Chapter number 34. ...

Readers, see Episode 2 to know how this story proceeds prior to Episode 3. See these Episode 2 chapters in the preceding book:

AND NOW READ ON....

As this Episode 3 Book tells us more about
how our characters, Risa, Gavon, Dan, and
now others they know — or think they know...
as well as the rest of us,
have found themselves and ourselves
here on the edge of a new reality,
a new world,
and likely also whole new levels of
personal and political,
romantic, psychological, biological,
economic, and political,
confusion and corruption.

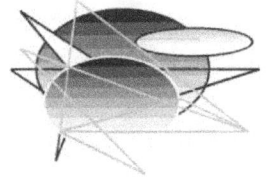

THE BLOODWIN CODE

EPISODE 3 BOOK

BLOODWIN CHRONICLES: VOLUME ONE

Episode 3, Part One

Chapter 34

DEAD REPLICANTS

Dr. Gavon DeScott of Bloodwin Labs...

... found himself dealing with an unexpected problem. He had to quickly squelch a minor rebellion, of all things. Several of his replicants had just then decided they would flee the confines and control of Bloodwin.

Their idea is entirely ridiculous, Gavon told himself. *These replicants have no money, no place to go, no legal names, no finger prints, no identification papers of any sort. And for that matter, they do not exist in society's terms. So they have not only nowhere to go, but no one to be.*

Yet, Gavon still had to put a stop to this situation right away, most definitely before Dr. Dan Williamson arrived and Dr. Risa Winters, his dear beloved Risa, returned. After all, Dan and Risa had no idea that sometimes some replicants attempted to go rogue. (Or so Gavon thought, as Risa had not told him she had met a rogue replicant). Dan and Risa also had no idea how very many replicants Gavon had made of himself. They also had no idea how Gavon handled such attempts at escape.

23

Gavon's solution was simple, and ready to implement. After all, he had had to order emergency actions like this before. He had already in place a procedure for signaling his guards to rapidly track and kill rogue replicants. So now, Gavon did just this.

It wasn't long before there were a number of dead replicants in the woods around the Bloodwin grounds. Upon being signaled, the guards had immediately tracked these rogue replicants, using the same transmitter functions planted inside all replicants, then located and shot these rogues. Some were shot directly, others killed by bullets fired from Bloodwin drones. Now the guards were quietly collecting these replicant bodies in order to put them in the incinerator at a remote end of the property.

Gavon was always clear with himself about this: rogue replicants had to go. There was no place in the Bloodwin Plan, and no place in the world, for replicants who chose to do something other than what they had been ordered to do. And of course, all orders, all decisions regarding the specific roles of the individual replicants, came from Gavon himself.

Gavon felt nothing regarding the termination of these rogue replicants. As he had explained to Risa, the death of one's replicant was as simple as getting a haircut. Although this was not exactly true in all cases, Gavon had not delved too deeply into the details of this. He had only told Risa what he wanted her to know at that time.

Gavon laughed for a moment as he recalled what his creator, the original Dr. Gavon DeScott, had once told him: *all replicants are created equal, but some are more equal than others.*

Gavon consoled himself with the truth he had created for himself: He, Gavon 2.0, was far more equal than any other of his replicants, as he was for all intents and purposes, *the* Gavon Senior, the original Gavon. He was the man who ran Bloodwin, who made all this possible, who in essence *was* Bloodwin. This is what the original Gavon, the real Dr. DeScott who had created all this, had wanted. Or, at least this is what Gavon 2.0, Gavon Junior posing as Gavon Senior, was telling himself Gavon Senior had wanted.

Gavon 2.0 was now, and for the foreseeable future, likely as long as he chose to be, likely forever if he had his way, commander in chief of all Bloodwin Enterprises and of the Bloodwin Code itself.

Chapter 35

EXTREMES IN PLACE

Dr. R. Winters update:

Deeper inside envelope. Continuing access to Bloodwin Project, business and lab/s. Far deeper inside now as far deeper cover required. Extremes in place. Possible procedural challenges to cover have been addressed. No questions re my presence and vetting. Entirely accepted into Bloodwin fold, actually now have been made a Bloodwin business partner. Further detailing info on primary subjects, business founders/clone designers DeScott and Williamson, who are inadvertently revealing in ever more depth their research agendas and international marketing scope and planning.

Will proceed to next steps: deeper under cover, deeper measures taken to record more fully the effects of Bloodwin's human replication developments on the mind, emotions as well as mental functioning—also on possible artificially induced breeding functions. Also note marketing agenda scope being investigated. China a key focus of Bloodwin. Moving into deeper cover now for increased protection of this investigation. Will contact you when next surface. Envelope sealed until further notice.

Risa stopped typing into the encryptor and hit send.

Somewhere else, at the Agency Risa was reporting to, a click sounded, signaling that an encrypted message had been sent in from her device. Risa could not know that there were actually two clicks, this one by the machine of her intended recipient at the Agency, and another click somewhere else.

The other click actually took place in China. Bloodwin's tendrils were already global, and even reaching into satellite communication functions. Risa had no idea that this other monitoring of her encrypted communications was also taking place, or at least attempting to. However, this second party, whoever it was, was unable to decrypt this communication.

Risa was definitely unaware of this second monitoring taking place, and definitely had no idea who was trying to monitor her communications. She just went on with what she was doing, proceeding with the messy work at hand, investigating Bloodwin.

Her decision not to report to the Agency everything she was finding out, and everything she was experiencing, continued. How could she even begin to explain how deeply in love she had fallen, albeit perhaps against her will and under the influence of Bloodwin compounds—Risa could not know for certain. Risa could not tell the Agency that she had fallen in love with the key subject, Dr. Gavon DeScott! *Well actually, with the number one replication of Dr. Gavon DeScott.*

Risa told herself she definitely could not tell her superiors at the Agency that Dr. DeScott was himself a replicant, the number one replicant the original Dr. DeScott had created to secure himself *technical immortality*, the very technical immortality Bloodwin Corporation had designed and was now selling at astronomical prices to key players around the world.

And of course, Risa also told herself that she could not tell her superiors at the Agency that she was now planning on spending the rest of her life with this man she had fallen madly and irreversibly in love with, this replicant of Dr. Gavon DeScott. She had to hide this obsession level stuff that had overtaken her life.

Of course, what Risa was hiding from herself was as big as what Risa was hiding from everyone else, wasn't it?

36

TRUTH WOULD COME OUT

Things worked as planned.

Dan arrived at Bloodwin Labs on time. When Gavon answered the door, he hugged his dear friend, and mentioned that he had just heard from Risa. Gavon told Dan the lie that he and Risa had agreed on. This way Dan would never guess that Risa was waiting at the other end of the property to appear to be arriving there for the first time, and arriving late. Now Gavon told Dan that Risa said she had taken a wrong turn, long before the guest house, due to the faulty mapping function, but was now on her way.

Deep inside, very deep inside, somewhere in his mind – or in *someone's* mind (Gavon Senior's?), he was not sure where, Gavon did feel some great regret about lying to Dan. However, against the backdrop of the larger lie to Dan, this was minor.

And the larger lie was a must right now. Despite his familiarity with this project, and most all of its ins and outs, Dan would not be able to handle knowing that its founder, Gavon

Senior, the original, was dead. This could destroy Dan. Or, was what could destroy Dan more likely that: Gavon Junior had been keeping the fact that Gavon Senior was gone a secret for quite some time now, for years?

Furthermore, Gavon kept reminding himself, Dan definitely had no idea regarding his own full lineage, what his full relationship to Gavon Senior actually was: *Gavon Senior was actually Dan's father!*

Dan had no idea that he actually was the son Gavon (Senior) had always wanted. Dan was definitely the son Gavon Senior had created from his own along with his beloved wife's genes: Gavon Senior had done this after his beloved wife had died young. And, Dan had no idea that Gavon Senior had made Dan his full and only heir—as Dan was indeed his only son, his only biological child. This was something about which Dan definitely had no idea.

It had been the responsibility of Gavon Junior to break the news of all this to Dan, when Dan was ready to handle it. Gavon Junior had promised Gavon Senior that he would. However, Gavon Junior had not yet found the right time, not even after all these years. Instead, he, Gavon Junior, had just stepped into Gavon Senior's shoes, with the change entirely unnoticeable to everyone, including Dan. Just doing that, and secretly incinerating Gavon Senior's body, was apparently what Gavon Senior himself had directed before he died; he had apparently not wanted his death disclosed at that time.

And Gavon Junior, as had been true for Gavon Senior, had been experimenting on himself, on *themselves*, with Bloodwin anti-aging compounds. Of course, Dan <u>did</u> know something about Gavon Senior's anti-aging work, as Gavon Senior himself had told Dan about this work, noting that these Bloodwin Anti-Aging Compounds (these BAAC's) would be worth a lot of money someday. So, Dan simply figured that Gavon Senior kept appearing not to age because of these anti-aging compounds. Dan never suspected that Gavon Senior had been replaced by a replicant of Gavon Senior.

What this means is that Dan had never wondered whether Gavon Junior, actually Gavon 2.0, was an imposter. This idea was the farthest thing from Dan's mind. Gavon was posing as Gavon Senior and Dan was not aware of this.

Dan believed the Gavon he worked with and loved was *the* Gavon, the original Gavon. This meant that Gavon Senior's number one replicant, Gavon Junior, was, for all intents and purposes, Gavon Senior to Dan. Of course, since Gavon Senior was still alive so far as Dan new, the word "Senior" had never been used. Neither had "Junior" or "Gavon 2.0."

Of course, all this did mean that Gavon 2.0 and *not* Dan knew *Dan was the full and only heir to all of Bloodwin*. Dan was the heir to Gavon's past, present, and future Bloodwin, to all the Bloodwin properties, possessions, inventions, designs, clients, funds, plans, and to all the Bloodwin fortune. As time had gone by, Gavon (Junior) had begun to wonder how all this would play out for him, the number one replicant of Gavon Senior.

What was most troubling for Gavon Junior was that, were Dan to find out he was heir to everything, this would mean *Dan would find out he actually owned Gavon Junior, as replicants were property, property of Bloodwin.*

Dan had no idea that all this was racing through Gavon's mind right then. Dan simply continued the conversation he thought they were having. "Good, Gavon. So, we have some time to talk about our greatly expanded financial foundation before Risa gets here," Dan said as he and Gavon moved into the elegant smoked cherry wood paneled conference room. "Risa should know about it all, as she is becoming a partner. She should know," Dan continued, "that is, if she doesn't yet know, that already twenty-five percent of the world's top one thousand wealthiest have signed up, and that many of their replication processes are actually already beginning."

Gavon thought to himself that Dan should, at some point, know that a few, quite a few, of these customers' replication processes had actually already been completed. In fact, full Bloodwin replicants were already walking the world, largely undetected.

But when should Dan be told this? Not yet, Gavon thought to himself. So here, today, Gavon just answered, "Yes. Agreed. Risa should know, soon, as she is partner. And, as you recall, when we discussed this meeting last week, we planned to move through a massive amount of material today."

Dan nodded, "Yes, we have to. Things are moving so quickly on all the levels of Bloodwin's work. It's great. I think we've got what should be presented ready, at least in terms of documents. Let's pull them out now."

The two men rapidly pulled their documents from the shelves around the conference table. They carefully lined everything up on the table to present in order. They were a great team, and highly organized, so this was easy.

They both ignored the painful issue of the two of them being in love with the same woman. Dan simply assumed Risa had rejected both of them now. Or at least Dan hoped this. *If I cannot have Risa, I sure do not want Gavon to have her either,* Dan quietly told himself. *I would do anything for Risa, including let her go, but would Gavon? I would do anything for this woman, give so much up for her, maybe even kill for her.* Dan heard himself and shut his thoughts down, feeling ashamed of this kind of inner dialog. Dan loved Gavon, dearly loved this man. Gavon was like a father to him, Dan reminded himself.

Dan now raised a key question. "But, we do have to decide right now, before Risa gets here, when to present Risa with the actual product, the proof of replication success, a replicant. What do you think, Gavon? Today, or wait a bit longer maybe? I mean, seeing a replicant can be shocking, even traumatic, for a person," Dan said.

Gavon managed not to reveal his internal disturbance here. Gavon wasn't going to tell Dan that Risa had already seen a replicant during her secret visit to Bloodwin, and that he, Gavon himself, was this replicant. And Gavon certainly wouldn't add that several Gavon replicants had ravaged Risa, as had Gavon 2.0.

In this moment, Gavon suddenly realized that he had forgotten to prepare his clones – the actual products, the proof of replication success—for this sort of business meeting with Risa.

Moreover, he had given most of them a seventy-two hour sleeping compound, in addition to the sleep command transmission. Too many of them had been activated, too many had had sex with Risa without his permission, and now, that very morning, some had even gone rogue, *or at least tried to go rogue*. ... Plus, presentation of these replicants, clones, would be, when it did take place, a formal introduction of one or more of the Gavons which Gavon told himself he had to prepare them for, and to choose which to prepare for this. Since at least two or three of them had ravaged Risa without knowing to tell her they were not the exact Gavon she thought they were, this was going to have to be arranged very carefully, Gavon told himself.

Dan had been waiting for Gavon's response. "Gavon? I was saying that maybe we should wait to show Risa a replicant, as seeing a replicant can be shocking."

Gavon realized he needed to answer Dan. "Yes, yes, I was thinking about what you just said. I agree. I think we need to go deeper into the business and the marketing side of all this today, and step Risa slowly into the full picture. Maybe next meeting, or, better still, let's wait a little longer, a few weeks more."

"Yes," Dan answered, relieved, then explained, "You know, even for me, with my particular background – if we can call it a background, the first meeting with replicants was a most unsettling experience. And I sort of knew what to expect. Something about one's first meeting with a full replicant, let alone a simple clone, is a double take experience. On the one hand, there is nothing unusual to note. On the other hand, there is nothing at all usual, that is, if one knows what one is meeting. Because, if one knows, then the whole thing threatens to take out one's mental organization. Now the world is not as it is, or was. And then, if the world is not as it is, or was, then the person meeting the replicant is not as he is, or was, either. Reality is entirely redefined. This confusion strikes hard."

Gavon looked at Dan quite sincerely sympathetically. *So Dan is trying to tell me what it is like for a non-replicant to meet a replicant. Or even for a hybrid to meet a replicant.* Gavon silently reminded himself that Dan was actually a GM-HYB, a genetically manipulated hybrid. *But, the science is saying that this GM-HYB is more of a human person that I am, than Gavon 2.0, the Gavon Junior, is, that I am just a replicant of a person, not exactly a person. I am going to have to change this science, this wrong dictum, but not sure how yet. After all, we replicants are people too, as least some of us are. I am.*

Dan had no idea what was going on in Gavon's mind. Dan was still talking. "You know what I mean. Yes?"

"I get it, yes," Gavon answered, although he realized he did not quite get it. He could not know what Dan's experience of being Dan was. But Gavon went on, "Of course, you, unlike others, more than knew what to expect. I told you what to expect, remember?" Gavon was lying here, continuing in his assumed role as the real and only Gavon (who would be Gavon Senior), who had carefully prepared Dan for the reality he was living, and for being in the Bloodwin world. This meant that Dan, being a hybrid and being a Bloodwin man, knew more about this that the average person out there.

"Yes you did, and thank you for taking such great care of me, for preparing me for my life," Dan told his dear Gavon, who was of course not really Gavon "Senior," but Dan did not know this. … "So, Gavon," Dan went on, "I did hear what you told me, and I appreciated the care you took to tell me. But there was still some kind of unexplainable nevertheless first time shock that went with all this. This was both about seeing a replicant for the first time, and then about me, about my own reality. … You helped me understand myself as the hybrid you have created. But there were and still are some things that are hard for me to adjust to, such as the reality that I can not compete. I felt then and still do feel so very inferior to the replicant level of excellence. To everyone's level of excellence. I feel lesser as a hybrid human."

Gavon looked at Dan with faint surprise. "Inferior? I would say that you were always and still are superior to everyone around you." Here Gavon repressed his intense envy of Dan, as Dan was more a real person by outsider standards than Gavon Junior was. Gavon told himself, *Well, Dan is real, I'll give him that, whatever real is. Dan is the actual offspring of Gavon Senior and his beloved wife. Raised in a lab, in essence a test tube baby, but still the actual genetic offspring. He is Gavon Senior's son. Sadly, I will never be.*

Suddenly Gavon Junior silently but sternly reminded himself that Dan was, in some ways, his <u>own son</u> as Dan was <u>the only</u> son of Gavon Senior. And, in some ways, Dan was, for Gavon (Junior), but not for Dan of course, the brother of Gavon Junior. This confusion made it difficult to know how to be with Dan. Fatherly? Brotherly? Friendly? Loving? Envious? Devious?

Still, Dan and Gavon were deeply connected. This connection continued to confuse Gavon. And Dan thought Gavon Junior was the Gavon Senior who had produced him in a lab. Dan had never seen Gavon Junior until it was time, as Gavon Senior had kept him hidden away until it was time for Gavon Junior to replace Gavon Senior. *An entirely seamless, unnoticed replacement,*

Gavon silently reminded himself. *Dan need never know. Should Dan ever know? But Gavon Senior wanted Dan to know, it is even in his Will.*

This was all so complicated. Dan still had no idea that his dear dear old friend and father-like mentor, Gavon Senior, was actually his true biological father, and was actually dead now for quite some time.

Could it ever be made right? Could Dan ever be told his father was dead? Could Dan ever be told his father was truly his father? How, after all this time? *Well, this cannot be done right now, not for a while, not yet. Dan definitely cannot know yet*, Gavon told himself, despite the fact that Dan had a right to know.

What would Dan do with the truth? Would Dan then assume control of all of Bloodwin, and of all of the Gavons--given that he would then know he had inherited all of them along with all of Bloodwin? Not at all desirable, should probably be prevented, Gavon silently advised himself right then and there. But again, he knew he loved Dan like a son, it was part of his programming to love Dan. He felt fatherly toward Dan. The original Gavon had wanted Gavon Junior to keep things together until Dan was ready to take over. But that was years ago.

The layer of lies was already so thick and complex. The question was how to untangle all this without harming his only son and brother, his dear friend, Dan. But some day, Dan would have to know all this and so much more, for many reasons. For example, that Dan was Gavon Senior's full and only heir would have to be known should anything happen to him, to Gavon Junior. The other Gavons should not just keep ownership and control of everything forever. *Should they?* They certainly weren't being prepared to. *Not exactly.*

And how much should Dan know about Risa? Gavon was also asking himself this. As he did, he realized all this was more and more tied together by the minute. Gavon was not only keeping key secrets from Dan, but also from Risa.

Could it be that Dan should never know any more about anything than he presently does, Gavon dared ask himself again and again these days…. *And for that matter, perhaps Risa should also never know everything.*

37

NOTHING UNUSUAL

Risa arrived a little late, as planned.

The meeting between the three of them, this gifted triangle born that last Saturday on the Bloodwin Yacht, went well. It was actually quite productive. Dan didn't seem to find anything too unusual about Risa's and Gavon's behavior. Of course, Dan could not help but wonder how they were doing and whether they were wondering how he was doing. *Do either of them really care about how I am doing*, Dan made sure he only silently asked himself.

Risa made certain she steered clear of asking to see any product samples, any replicants, and carefully focused on other matters. "So, the numbers work. And I am beginning to feel quite conversant in much of this, the mechanisms of the product. I'm going to need to see the alpha, beta, and general outcome data summaries. I want to know all the stats through and through."

And somehow it all went smoothly. In fact, the three of them were definitely hugely excited about the work. They together resonated around these plans for making this revolutionary product available and ready to change the course of history, of society, of the global economy, and of every part of life on this planet. At one point, they even noted that what Bloodwin was offering was also a means of making longer distance space travel effective, even fun. Just pack and freeze, and rotate in and out, one's replicants. Technical immortality would have great uses, both on- and off- planet.

Ultimately, all three of them, including Risa, realized that Bloodwin's great power was expanding day by day. Already Bloodwin was collecting and beginning to store the brain and gene maps of a quarter or more of the world's wealthiest and most powerful people. In fact, some of their replication materials were already fully recorded and stored at a distant, top secret and fully fire-walled, Bloodwin location.

No one else, no other company or team, should ever get their hands on these brain and gene maps, or generate their own library of powerful people's brain waves and information bits including thought and personality patterns, gene maps, genetic-environment responses, and memories.

And of course, control of the assets of these persons to preserve these for their replicants was also protected information, held by the also offshore and quite secret Bloodwin Bank.

Risa posed as having to leave early, having pressing commitments back home. Dan did not guess that Risa was trying to appear to be leaving, while she was not really leaving, she was coming back later to be with her lover, that man she simply could not stay away from, Gavon.

Dan simply decided Risa wanted to put the madness of the last weekend completely behind her and get on with her life.

The three of them set a date to next meet back there, all together. Dan drew Risa a map so that she could be sure not to get lost on the way back to the freeway. He did secretly write in small letters, in the lower corner of this map, "call me," hoping she would see this later. However, it would be much much later that she would finally call. And that day would hurt.

Risa left. She headed out the long driveway, and purposefully, once out of view of Bloodwin, took the wrong turn. Today, she did not take the convertible top down. She wanted no one to notice her. She drove out a back road into the hills rather than to the freeway.

About fifteen minutes into the drive, she saw a countryside park and pulled into its parking lot. This would be a good place to wait, and to rest while she waited to return to Gavon. She saw a small building and drove her car behind it to hide. She told herself this was silly, as Dan would never head this way. But then she told herself that, *one can never be too sure of anything.* So she stayed in her car, parked behind this building, and waited for time to pass.

From her car, she could see a playground where about a dozen children were playing, watched by what was either a parent, or babysitter or nanny or some other adult. Risa stared at the children, grateful for this momentary distraction. She so much needed a distraction. The adult there seemed to Risa more like a caretaker than a parent. Perhaps this was because there were so many children, more than were typical of the usual family size these days. Yet the children looked related, quite similar in appearance. *They are probably siblings,* Risa mused. *Maybe there are some twins or triplets among these siblings. ... A lot of children for one family, though,* Risa told herself again. *Maybe some are cousins. Cousins can look a lot alike as well.* Risa distracted herself from herself by watching these lovely children play.

The picture of these siblings playing suddenly reminded Risa of her own two children. Right away, despite the drug she was on making her highly rational and not very emotional, she started to sob loudly, quickly closing her car window so no one would hear. She cried and cried. The tears continued to flow for maybe five minutes until she had exhausted herself. She stared sadly at the children, longing for her own. She was so overcome with sadness that she did not realize these children actually all looked exactly the same. Therefore, she did not wonder about this interesting coincidence.

She locked her car doors, reclined the seat of her car, and closed her eyes to take a nap. She was so tired. But she couldn't sleep, so she just laid there with her eyes closed. She could hear the children shouting and laughing, which made her all the more homesick for her own children. Was she breaking her own heart by choosing Gavon over her children? *Too late,* she told herself. *No turning back. I have been forever changed by all that has happened in the past few days. There is no going back.*

Maybe she dozed, she was not sure. Time passed, perhaps half an hour. She awoke abruptly when a loud noise pulled her out of her rest. She opened her eyes and looked around quite nervously. But this noise turned out to be merely a car engine, that of a van, nothing for Risa to worry about, nothing near Risa's car.

She watched sadly as the last of the children in the park were led into the elegant van, finding herself longing more for her own children. It was as if she was getting back in touch with her own suppressed yet very natural motherly emotions.

The van's doors were closing, and the adult got in. Risa watched carefully, trying to distract herself from her own thoughts.

It turned out there was a driver as well as this nanny or whatever she was. The van was indeed an elegant van, a long limo-like van, probably with all the hi-tech comforts inside. *Probably a very wealthy family*, Risa mused. She watched as the van headed out of the park, staring at it, wishing she could see her own children for just a moment right then.

Risa was glad that her children were with her dear husband, Harvey. This was reassuring. He was a great father. *Oh my God, Harv, what will I say to you when I see you?*

As the van rolled out of the park, Risa saw that it had the usual California plates, and some kind of name of a school or something painted in small letters on the back. *Probably a fancy boarding school, wonder which one*, Risa mumbled. She squinted curiously, trying to read the name of the school or whatever it was as the luxurious van pulled out of the parking lot.

She sat up straight when she made out the words on the back of the van: Bloodwin Corporation.

<u>38</u>

NOTHING USUAL

Gavon texted:

"All clear. Everything went well. Come back to me my love, love of my life. Come back now. I have to have you."

Risa texted back, "Be there in about an hour, my love."

Risa felt a combination of great relief, rising desire (as the desire reduction drug Gavon had given her was wearing off), and a vague sort of looming but nevertheless subtle apprehension.

Seeing those children get into a Bloodwin-labelled van had been an unwanted surprise. Was this just a strange coincidence? But Bloodwin was such an uncommon name. Could there maybe be a Bloodwin boarding school or children's home? What would Bloodwin be doing with a school? Seeing children associated in any way with all this Bloodwin stuff, all this with Gavon who she was stepping so far over the line for, was a lot to digest. Could this be a deal breaker? She didn't know. She hoped not.

Risa decided to sit a while longer and try to digest everything. She began thinking about all of this using the intellectual parts of her brain. Yet, as the minutes went by, she found her thoughts giving way to her feelings, especially her physical feelings, sexual cravings, for Gavon. That four hour desire-numbing drug Gavon had given her was indeed beginning to wear off. And, Risa was not going to take another pill right now. Therefore, Risa's overwhelming desire for Gavon was trumping her apprehension.

Soon, she was ready to head back. She had to head back, she had to have Gavon. Sure, she would ask him about the children, at a good time. Yet, the whole shocking matter was now rapidly receding in priority. Loving Gavon was most important. She wanted him so much right now. Her, or someone's, biochemistry, was running wild again.

She drove back to Bloodwin as quickly as she could, speeding with desire. Every second that went by was another second without Gavon. She found herself reliving their love making, and feeling increasingly desperate for more. Again, and even more than ever, each cell in her body was craving this man, Gavon. This man, or whatever he was, replicant of a man....

She arrived at Bloodwin earlier than she had expected, parked her car, and raced to the door. There she took a deep breath, tried to quickly neaten her hair, and then reached for the bell. As had happened before, in the few moments before she could actually ring the bell, the door opened.

She saw Gavon standing there, looking wonderful, magnetic, and appearing only faintly surprised.

"Gavon," Risa whispered.

He stared deeply into her beautiful dark eyes, in his way of making close contact. He gazed very deeply into her core. Piercingly deep.

"Gavon," was all Risa could say. He was as fabulous as she remembered him. More fabulous by the minute.

He pulled her inside and closed the door.

They stood there, completely immobile and so very silently, as their eyes fixed on each other. No need to speak. Frozen, the sexual heat between them was as immediate and fierce as it had been, even more so now, this sexual heat the captor and they the prisoners, taking direction. *Sheer biochemical direction.*

Gavon grabbed her by the hand and led her to the bedroom where they had spent so many delightful hours. They began to tear at each other's clothes. It could not have been longer than a few seconds before Gavon was on top of Risa, holding her and kissing her most passionately. She hugged him as he did so, her body flushing to that high heat she had come to know was part of all this. She knew any moment they would be making that unreal, almost unbelievable, wildly passionate and wildly pounding love. She would be screaming uncontrollably with extreme absolute pleasure, the pleasure of a lifetime, of all lifetimes. As the white hot sexual elation of anticipation was now flowing into her veins, racing through her blood stream, filling her every cell with an unheard of level of ecstasy, somewhere in the mansion a door slammed.

Gavon froze a moment and then jumped up. He quickly grabbed his clothes and left the room as he dressed.

Some kind of emergency, Risa figured, her longing for Gavon still increasing as the minutes went by. But then more minutes went by, and Risa began to be concerned something was keeping Gavon from her.

Gavon returned, fully dressed.

It took but a moment for Risa to realize he was not wearing what he had worn when he had left the room a while ago. And it took just one more moment for Risa to realize what had happened.

"Oh God!!!!!" Risa shouted as she pulled a blanket around herself and jumped out of bed.

"Wait, my dear, wait," Gavon begged.

"NO!!!! WHO WAS THAT JUST NOW!!!!! WHO!!!!! YOU? OR NOT YOU?" Risa was angry, even verging on furious.

Gavon grabbed Risa and wrapped his arms around her gently but forcefully. She tried hard to wriggle free but could not. "Listen to me, please listen," Gavon pleaded. "I love you."

"Let me go!" Risa demanded.

"Of course I will let you go, my dearest, and please can you calm down," Gavon responded gently as he kissed her shoulder.

Sexual desire raced through Risa. That irrepressible white hot longing raced through her veins again. She reasoned with herself that this could not be so bad, it could not be so bad because it felt so damn good.

"Risa, please let me talk to you, please." Gavon had forgotten to go back and give the last one of his clones, replicants, the sleeping transmission and drug. That replicant had already been asleep (*or at least had appeared asleep*) when he gave it to the rest of them. And that replicant had still been asleep (*or at least had appeared still asleep*) when Gavon checked him later. Should he share information about this sloppy mistake with Risa? And, could he tell Risa he was wondering whether one of his own replicants had fooled him, posed as asleep in order not to be put to sleep? No, this would raise the matter of punishment that might be necessary. *This is far too much to share with Risa,* Gavon told himself.

Risa was quiet for a moment while she struggled to regain control of her emotions. She told herself insistently that she had to get a grip because this was part of loving Gavon with all her heart. She had to accept this sort of experience. He meant her no harm, he loved her so very very much. And, if she was honest with herself, it turned her on so unbelievably much. If having one incredibly amazing Gavon was the peak of ecstasy, what would more than one incredibly amazing Gavon be?

Risa eventually relaxed in his arms as her breathing slowed. She finally said, "OK, I am OK, and I will sit down so we can talk." *And make love again,* she told herself, as she also told herself _no_, she would not make love with him again.

They sat as Risa just looked at Gavon's now very sad face. Eventually she spoke, "Gavon, please, please help me with this. I am just not sure I can step over this line. I am just not sure I can sanely get myself to do this with the other ones of you. That was what was happening to me, wasn't it? Wasn't it? It was, wasn't it?"

Gavon now had tears in his own eyes. "Yes Risa, it was. I had thought you would be here a half hour or more later, and I wanted to run to the little store in town, to buy you flowers and candy. I should have sent someone else, I should have."

"... One of the other Gavons you mean? Send one of the other Gavons to buy me flowers?" Risa was trying to think about this, but for some reason her emotions were too rocky. "I do not want flowers from any of them."

"Risa," I would never harm you, nor would any of my copies. As I have said, we are all me. If this is all too much for you, I will be devastated, in great pain forever, lonely and alone the rest of my life. But if you need me to, as I've said, I *will* get out of your life for good. ... And by the way, I will make sure you always see profits from your share of this business, no matter what you decide now or in the future."

"Gavon, you are so honorable, I hear this. But no. No, do not leave my life, please do not even go there. You know I couldn't bear it. We just have to arrange a way soon, very soon, for me to be able to ask who is with me, who is who. And to be able to stop things if I cannot take it." She thought to herself, *What woman would turn down having this man so totally in love with her, and having spare copies of him whenever he was busy?* She was working to accept this. She was also working to understand how it was that she could not do anything <u>but</u> accept this.

Gavon figured as much and suggested, "Or, you could let yourself make love with one of my replicants again, so that you could again see it is as wonderful with each of us, and that we all love you, and that we are all me. I would again be envious, and longing for you so very much, but I would deal with it, because I would feel it all, every bit of it." *Well, almost every bit of it, for now,* Gavon added silently, *as the full transmission synching functions are not fully up and running yet. … Replicant management is an art in itself,* Gavon was telling himself. *Replicant synching is still being perfected.*

Gavon realized that the number of secrets he was keeping from his dear Risa was increasing.

Risa was silent for a while, while her sexual longing heated to new levels. She was in awe of what she was experiencing. Ecstatic sex and love with more than one Gavon! A Gavon available to her whenever she wanted one! She could do this, she could make love with one of the others, she could, she told herself. She was feeling an almost overwhelming longing as she considered trying this. After all, she had already made fabulous love with two or three of the other clones, replicants, whatever they were. *Yes OTHER, as Gavon number one is also a clone,* she reminded herself.

Gavon spoke softly now. "Risa, let me send him in to you. He will be very good to you, and I will wait in my office. We have to get this handled at some point, because it could happen again, and I do not want you near a breakdown again."

"… Will he be the one that was here just now, right here in this bed?" She found that she still wanted *him*, perhaps even *him* in *particular*, she could not tell. Perhaps she should find out.

"Do you want that one, my dear Risa?"

"I am pretty nervous about this, really, I mean, what will this be like? What will this do to us? Would I be breaking your heart? Or will this be you, for all intents and purposes *you*, and make no difference to you?" *And make no difference to me, as I would love it, I admit it,* Risa chided herself. She decided right then that there were parts of all this, such as her sheer enjoyment of this multiple lover situation, that she would not talk about with Gavon. *Gavon is a very powerful man, with immense physical and mental strength, a man I would never want to anger or for that matter make very jealous. That is, if replicants can be very angry or even very jealous. Who knows,* she told herself.

"This will be me, for all intents and purposes. For this reason, this will not break my heart. I can experience this." In any case, Gavon had already had practice at this, as his copies had already been with Risa. Gavon had realized, very quickly, that this had to be all right. Now that he had found the love of his life, the woman he had to spend his life with, he would have to help her (and himself) get used to this reality. He would be patient and love her every step of the complex but delicious way. He would find a way to tolerate his replicants loving Risa. Just a few of them, only the ones he trusted. He would find a way to make the experience of this work for him. *And for Risa, too,* he told himself.

"Oh gee, Gavon, I am wondering about the sanity of all this. ... Really, I just cannot yet think entirely clearly about what this means. And, I'm not going to be a big chicken, so I say all right. I might as well work through this. So now, what happens next?"

Risa was astounded at her readiness to do what was one of the most out of the normal things a person could do. She could feel the level of sexual desire increasing within her with each passing second. Her heart was on fire. White heat was filling her veins. More white heat than ever. A penultimate longing, craving, like no other.

"Let me kiss you, start to love you, and then let me leave and send him in to you. He will pick up exactly where I leave off. You won't know the difference."

Frightening, disturbing, but totally irresistibly exciting, what an awesome turn on, Risa had to admit to herself. *Impossible to say no to.* "Alright," she whispered. She almost invited Gavon to come back and watch, but she wasn't ready for anything like this yet. Of course, she shivered inside, he would be watching in another way, via transmitter, right?

Gavon took her hand, took her back to the bed, and began to kiss her lips and face. The already heightened passion grew as they did. At a certain moment, Gavon said, "Stay here, I will be right back," and left the room quickly. As he did, he almost turned around and stayed. *But too late, now I have to let this happen, damn it, damn it, damn it,* Gavon told himself. He was treading into new territory here, even for himself. *Look, it is clear here that we replicants do definitely have powerful feelings, real emotions, just like Humans do.*

Risa shook with extreme excitement, the highest level of icy hot excitement yet. This was really happening!!! She was about to melt with anticipation when Gavon returned. Or, *a* Gavon returned. He pulled off his clothes and resumed the passionate embrace.

Risa, so profoundly and inescapably exhilarated by all this, said nothing and went along with it all. Eventually, when the white hot desire was almost too much for Risa, they moved into the wildest lovemaking yet.

They did not stop for hours. Hours and hours. When they did, they closed their eyes next to each other, very still, embracing, and fell asleep.

About an hour later, Risa began to awake, awash in the ecstasy of an unbelievable, almost divine, new level of sexual bliss. There was something about this that had exceeded every other loving making even thus far. Risa did not want to let this feeling fade away. It was too good. Finally Risa opened her eyes. The man that had been in the bed was gone. Or was he?

Gavon, a Gavon, was sitting in a chair on the side of the bed, looking at her, almost studying her. He had placed a vase with bright flowers beside the bed. He had brought in a pitcher with juice and a platter of cheeses and fruit.

Risa sat up and looked around. She attempted to smile, and did so rather faintly. "Are you Gavon?" she said. "_The_ Gavon? _My_ Gavon?"

"Yes, I am Gavon, the Gavon, your Gavon. Can I give you something to drink or eat?" Gavon was measuring his own response to this situation, checking in with himself on how he was handling the reality that the love of his life had just made passionate love with another man--well, not a man, a replicant. The synching and transmission functions had not worked well, so Gavon had to feel what he imagined he would be feeling based on his recent experiences of sexual passion with Risa. This was almost enough. Gavon suppressed his internal response to another man having his woman. He told himself that this was Gavon Senior's jealously, not his own.

She nodded yes, as she was hungry.

And they ate together, calmly, and touching each other every few moments. Risa was not sure what to say, and now felt a bit of embarrassment. She felt somewhat as if she had just cheated on Gavon. However, Gavon seemed all right, a little distant, but alright. Eventually Gavon warmed up to her, and eventually Risa relaxed.

This whole thing was the new emotional territory of the emerging clone and replicant reality, and would go into Risa's report to the Agency. Or would it?

After a while, although Gavon now desperately craved sexual time with Risa, he felt he should wait. He asked Risa if she would like to take a walk with him. She nodded yes, and then he very carefully helped her finish dressing. As he did, he eyed her beautiful body, her dark skin now glowing like he had never seen it do. He wanted this woman, this body, this person, he wanted every bit of *her*. She was everything to him. She was the ultimate joy in his life. And, he had, although a little against his will, realized that it was immensely sexually exciting for him to have one of his top replicants ravish Risa, and to ravish her beyond all expectations. This was not only OK, it was great. Fabulous, maximum ecstasy. *Supra-hyper maximum approval level*, Gavon told himself.

He also told himself that, while this could be a selling point for his Bloodwin Personal Replication Services, he would have to be careful how this was presented to potential clients. Clients would need to be carefully prepared for experiences like this. *Or they might murder their replicants*, Gavon secretly told himself. *Or the reverse perhaps could also happen*. Gavon knew this based on what he was experiencing.

As the next few minutes went by, both Gavon and Risa could feel that their extreme love, and their extreme passion, for each other had now deepened to a new, ever more profound level. This entire event had taken them to this new level. As always, every second of their togetherness was better than the last. This new dimension only made everything already so wonderful even better.

It was several hours before they actually talked about what had happened. By then, Risa had more than made her peace with it. It now made sense to her. This whole world she had entered, this place where it was so all or nothing, this was all part of loving Gavon with all her heart and flesh and soul. And she did. She did. She did. She was sure she did. At least she thought she did.

Too soon for either of them, they came to the end of that emotional, loving, wild and passionate week plus a few extra days (while Risa had waited for Harvey to text her with the all clear from the doctor treating him and her children, caring for them while they had the mega-measles).

Risa had made her peace with the world of Bloodwin. Gavon the original had extended his life through this Gavon replicant she was with, this primary Gavon, Gavon 2.0. Risa's Gavon was Gavon in every way, just a fresher newer version. The extremely high intelligence, genius, and character of the original Gavon were all there, present in this Gavon Risa loved.

And there were other Gavons, all controlled and directed by the primary Gavon, Risa's Gavon. These were fine men, they were no different from Risa's Gavon, except that they were not in charge. Risa's Gavon was in charge, only Risa's Gavon. Still, in essence, they were all Risa's Gavon.

This was all fine. Risa had not only made peace with all this, she had fully understood it and fully agreed to it. In fact, all the Gavons, because of their programming, were programmed to love Risa and only Risa. *What more could any woman want? Seriously, what more,* Risa asked herself.

At the same time, Risa made a mental note that somehow this had to go into her report to the Agency. They needed to know about this Bloodwin effect on the mind, heart, and soul for that matter. Was it the Bloodwin compounds or the replicant effect itself? But how would Risa be able to report on this without revealing her own over involvement? *Over* involvement was putting it more than mildly.

Gavon had even respected Risa's decision not to be cloned, replicated, synched or not synched, or at least to wait until she felt fully ready emotionally to go ahead.

"Respected" was putting it mildly, as Gavon had not respected any of this. *None of this is Risa's decision, not really. But don't think about this right now, as it would be dangerous to hint at this issue in any way,* Gavon reminded himself.

Gavon had expressed his profound and all-encompassing love for Risa. This was absolute unwavering love on all levels, love that would do whatever it took to make Risa's choices work for her, putting her first at all times. *Or at least appearing to.*

Gavon would select his best and most loyal replicants to help keep Risa sexually satisfied, enthralled, addicted, tied into the plan. He had to keep drugging Risa, as this would be necessary, as her sexual and emotional engagement was essential and of course much desired for that matter. That made sense to Gavon Junior as he was so totally in love. Risa was now his forever, according to plan.

39

SPECIAL SCHOOL

She had finally asked about ...

… and Gavon had gladly explained, the Bloodwin limo-van full of children. Risa found herself appreciating this knowledge and proud that Bloodwin had this going on.

There was indeed a Bloodwin boarding school. It was a special and wonderful school, a secret and unregistered school. Here, children of Bloodwin, children whose births were not registered anywhere other than at Bloodwin, were loved, cared for, protected, and provided the best education anywhere in the world. These children were being allowed, for various reasons such as socialization processing, to undergo the normal, or something like the normal, child and teen developmental stages. They were being allowed to develop their own minds, at least for now.

Children like these could not be in regular schools, as they were Bloodwin clones and replicants, and also hybrids, and others like them. Some of Bloodwin's engineered human beings, the

EHBs, also had to be protected like this. Some of these EHBs could not be turned out into the world. Other of Bloodwin's EHBs could be and had been for various reasons.

Obviously, the Bloodwin boarding school children were not the Bloodwin replicants grown directly to adulthood by the special acceleration and synching methods Bloodwin had developed. As Risa now knew, the accelerated replicants became adults almost immediately. On the other hand, the particular child clones at the boarding school were raised through at least some of the full cycle of child and teen development, raised to serve varying purposes which required somewhat normal pathways of child and teen development.

There was nothing so-called "normal" about these young people, however.

In fact, these children were all informed of their specific purposes. And each of these special children was being trained to fully understand all aspects of the Bloodwin project. They were *Bloodwin Beings*, a population serving and becoming part of the *Nation of Bloodwin*.

After Gavon had explained all this, it was time for Risa to leave. At that time, she and Gavon both drugged themselves with Gavon's special calming and desire reduction compound. This made Risa's departure possible. They had worked out a plan which required her to be at Bloodwin two nights a week for business purposes, and also sometimes to meet Gavon in a hotel closer to Risa's family home. Risa left with a large bottle of the pills that would help her subdue her longing for and response to Gavon, except when it was safe to feel the full explosive, fiery, absolutely wildly passionate, addictive, range.